FAMOUS ANIMAL STORIES

SCAT
The Movie Cat

By Justin F. Denzel

Illustrated by Herman B. Vestal

GARRARD PUBLISHING COMPANY
CHAMPAIGN, ILLINOIS

Copyright © 1977 by Justin F. Denzel
All rights reserved. Manufactured in the U.S.A.
International Standard Book Number: 0-8116-4861-3
Library of Congress Catalog Card Number: 77-23300

SCAT
The Movie Cat

Suddenly Scat the cat found herself in the water. A huge wave had crashed across the deck and had washed her overboard. She came up gasping for air.

The fishermen on the boat were busy fighting the storm. They did not know that Scat was gone.

Scat swam and swam. The waves rose almost as high as mountains all around her. Then she saw an empty fishbox floating on the water. Using her last bit of strength, she climbed into the box.

She held onto the box as hard as she could as it bobbed and rolled on the waves.

All night long the storm went on. It pushed the little box into Gull Harbor Bay.

In the morning the storm was over, and a warm Florida sun came up over the palm trees.

Scat looked around. She could see land, but she was too tired to swim.

Then she saw a boy in a small boat. He stopped every few minutes to pull up a crab trap.

Scat watched as the boy came closer. When he was next to the floating box, he saw the cat. Gently he lifted Scat into the boat.

"Hello, cat," he said. "I don't know how you got into that old fishbox, but it's a lucky thing for you that I came along."

Scat heard the words. She didn't know what they meant. Yet they sounded kind and friendly.

The collar that Scat was wearing was tight and water-soaked. The boy cut it off. He looked at the name scratched on the back. "So you're Scat," he said. "That's a pretty good name for a lost cat."

Next he cut some bait into small pieces. He held them out to the cat. But Scat was too weak to eat.

The boy rowed back to shore. He tied up his boat in front of an old beach cottage. A lady came out on the porch to meet him. "You're home early, Joel," she said.

"Yes, Granny," the boy replied. "Look what I found out on the bay."

The old woman took Scat in her arms. "Why the poor little thing is wet and frightened. She must have fallen overboard from a passing boat."

"Her name is Scat," said Joel. "It was marked on her collar."

"Then you'll have to put up a notice on the board down at the docks," said Granny. "Someone may be looking for her."

Joel nodded. "I tried to feed her some fish, but she won't eat. Do you think she is sick?"

Granny put the cat in a box lined with newspaper. She warmed some milk on the stove. When it was ready, she set it in front of the cat.

Scat was very tired, but she did take a few laps of the warm milk.

Granny smiled. "I'm sure she'll be all right," Granny said.

She was right. In a few days Scat could eat again. Soon she was a healthy, playful cat. Scat loved her new home. It was different from all the other places she had lived.

Scat had been born in the warehouse belonging to a local fruit company two years before. There she grew up and learned to catch rats and mice.

Then the fruit company closed. All the

workers left. There were no mice left to catch, so Scat wandered from place to place. No one seemed to want her. She ate whatever she could find.

One day she found her way down to the docks. There was the food she liked best, scraps of fish and crabmeat.

She sometimes went aboard the boats. The fishermen never chased her away. They often took her on fishing trips. And that is how Scat became a seagoing cat.

But now she was happy in her new home with Joel and Granny. They loved her and wanted to take care of her. Here there was lots of old furniture to scratch on. She could play with the lace on the curtains or climb up the stair

railing. And the porch was a good place to lie down and sleep in the sun.

Scat and Joel became the best of friends. She followed the boy wherever he went. She went with him when he pulled in his crab traps. She followed him to the Gull Harbor market to sell his catch.

There she walked through the long wooden sheds. She found bits of crab-meat and small fish. On the way home Joel often stopped at the ice-cream stand to buy a popsicle. He always saved a little for Scat.

Best of all Scat liked to go fishing. Joel sat on the pier. Scat sat on the post beside him.

After Joel caught a big fish, he would

put on a smaller hook and catch a little one for Scat. Scat learned to reach out and grab it with her paw.

It was a good life, and Joel and Scat were happy.

Joel had put a big sign on the board down at the docks. Days passed and no one came to claim Scat. Joel was glad.

But there were days that were not so good. Those were the days when Mr. Wozel came. Mr. Wozel owned the little cottage where Joel, Granny, and Scat lived. He came every month to collect the rent.

Mr. Wozel was a grumpy little man. One day he saw Scat sunning herself on the porch. "Shoo!" he said. "Get out of here."

Scat ran down the steps and hid in the beach grass.

"I don't want any cats around," said Mr. Wozel. "They're lazy animals, and it costs money to feed them."

"Only a few pennies," said Granny.

"If you have enough money to feed a cat," said Mr. Wozel, "how can you be so far behind in your rent?" Granny thought it best to say nothing.

After Mr. Wozel left, Granny told Joel, "It will be best if you keep Scat away from the house when Mr. Wozel comes around."

Scat had become a beautiful cat. Her fur was a rich reddish brown. With her bold black stripes, she looked like a little tiger.

One morning Joel and Scat were fishing from the pier. Joel watched while a man took pictures of a young woman. She was pretty, with long red hair almost the color of Scat's.

When the lady saw Scat, she said, "My, what a beautiful cat. May we take her picture?"

Joel nodded.

The man took a picture of Scat. Then the lady held Scat in her arms. The man took a picture of both of them.

When Joel got home, he told Granny all about it.

"Maybe Scat's picture will be on a postcard," said Granny.

Months went by. One afternoon Granny was looking at a magazine. On the cover

was a picture of the pretty lady. She was holding Scat in her arms.

"Well, what do you know," said Granny. "That's Lily DelRay, the famous movie star."

Joel was proud of his beautiful cat. He held the picture for Scat to see. "Look, Scat," he said. "It's your picture with the pretty lady."

Scat said, "Meow," and went over to her dish of sardines.

People all over the country saw the picture of Scat and Lily DelRay. Now Scat was known from coast to coast.

One day a man drove up to Granny's house. He wanted to buy Scat for Miss DelRay. "She'd like Scat to be in the movies," he said.

Joel shook his head. "Miss DelRay is a nice lady, but I love Scat too much to give her up."

"We would pay you a lot of money," said the man. "You could buy everything you want, even another cat."

"No," said Joel. "I don't think Scat would like to go away."

The man looked at Joel holding Scat in his arms. He smiled. "I see what you mean," he replied. "And I'm sure Miss DelRay will understand."

After the man left, Granny put her arm around Joel. "We wouldn't trade Scat for anything," she said.

The news of Scat's fame was the talk of Gull Harbor. Everyone knew she was a valuable cat.

A few days later Joel and Scat were fishing down at the pier. A big seaman came along. He wore boots, and he had a bag under his arm.

"Why, there you are, my little pet," he said, looking at Scat. "I've been hunting all over for you."

Joel was surprised.

"That cat belongs to me," said the man. "She fell off my boat the night of the big storm."

Joel picked Scat up in his arms. He was sure the man was lying. Everyone knew he had found Scat floating out on the bay.

"I don't believe you," said Joel. "I've had Scat for a long time now. You never came looking for her before."

"Well, I've come now," said the man. He grabbed Scat from Joel's arms and dropped her into the big bag.

Scat could not see anything. It was dark inside the bag. She scratched and tried to get out. All she could hear were Joel's angry cries as the man took her away.

A short while later the seaman took the bag aboard a boat. He dropped it in a corner below the deck. Scat heard the sound of water splashing. She knew she was on a boat.

Scat began to chew the side of the bag. She managed to make a small hole. She scratched and chewed. The hole got bigger and bigger.

Scat knew that the boat had started

to move. She heard the sound of the motor. Wildly she clawed at the hole. Soon it was large enough for her to get her head out. She looked around. In the darkness she saw the outlines of the steps leading to the upper deck.

The sound of the motor grew louder. The boat was leaving the dock. Scat pushed and tugged. Finally she got out of the bag. Without stopping she ran up the steps. She raced across the deck.

The big seaman saw her. He reached out to grab Scat's tail. But he missed. "Come back here, you little rascal," he shouted.

It was too late. Scat was already over the rail. She jumped with all her might and landed on the dock, six feet away.

All night long Joel lay awake worrying about Scat. Toward morning he heard a meow. He got up and looked out. There was Scat, sitting on the porch, looking up at the window. He ran down and picked her up.

"Scat's back," Joel yelled to Granny, as he hugged the cat in his arms.

After that Granny decided to let Joel keep Scat in the house. "She will be safer," said Granny.

One day, while Granny was shopping, Mr. Wozel came to the house. He was friendly and smiling. "Here's that lucky cat of ours," he said, patting Scat on the head.

"I thought you didn't like cats," said Joel.

"A person has a right to change his mind," said Mr. Wozel, "when the cat is as famous as Scat."

Joel said nothing.

"I understand Scat has a chance to be in the movies," said Mr. Wozel.

"Yes," said Joel. "But she's not going. I'm sure she wouldn't want to leave Gull Harbor."

"Sure," said Mr. Wozel, "as long as she has a good home like this. But what if she had no place to live?"

"What do you mean?" asked Joel.

"Granny owes me three months rent," said Mr. Wozel. "If she can't pay, I'll have to put her out. Then Scat won't have a home anymore."

Joel was so surprised. He could not

believe what was happening. "We'll get the money somehow," he said.

"Well now," said Mr. Wozel, "if Scat were in the movies, she'd make lots of money. Then Granny wouldn't have to worry."

"But that would mean Scat would have to go to Film City. I might never see her again," Joel said.

Mr. Wozel shook his head. "Oh, she'd only be gone five or six months. That's not so long."

"You mean I would get Scat back again?" asked Joel.

"Sure," said Mr. Wozel. "As soon as she makes a few pictures."

Joel was quiet for a moment. To him six months seemed like forever.

"You promise Scat will be home in six months?"

"I promise."

Joel almost choked on the words.

"Then I guess you can take her," he said sadly.

When Granny learned what Joel had done, she was angry. "Mr. Wozel's been talking about putting us out for years," she said.

"But he promised to bring Scat back in six months," said Joel.

Granny shook her head. She didn't believe a thing Mr. Wozel said.

Scat soon found herself on a plane headed for Film City. There Mr. Wozel took her to Miss DelRay.

Miss DelRay was delighted. She picked

Scat up and held the kitten against her cheek. "What a wonderful kitty," she said. "She's the most beautiful cat in the world."

Then she turned to Mr. Wozel. "Are you sure it's all right with Joel?"

"When the boy heard that Scat would be in the movies, he was more than happy to let her go," said Mr. Wozel.

Miss DelRay smiled. "You will be sure to pay Joel well for his kindness?" she asked.

"Why, of course I will," said Mr. Wozel. "As Scat's manager I promise you that everything will be just fine."

But everything was not fine with Scat. Scat didn't like all the petting and hugging. And she didn't like the smell of

Miss DelRay's perfume either. It made her sneeze.

The apartment had thick carpets that caught in Scat's claws. The tables and chairs were new and fancy. She missed the old ones at Granny's house, where she could scratch and climb.

There were no window sills to sit on. There was no porch on which to lie in the sun. Worst of all, the fish were in a large glass bowl.

Once Miss DelRay caught Scat trying to catch a fish with her paw. "No, no," she said. "You must not hurt the little fishes."

Outdoors there was nothing but tall buildings and noisy streets filled with traffic.

Instead of going fishing Scat often was taken to the beauty shop. It was called the Paws and Claws. Here she was given to a young lady in a white uniform. Her fur was carefully combed and brushed. She was sprayed with a perfume that made her smell like a flower garden.

She didn't like it when they cleaned her ears with a cotton stick. It tickled her all over and made her shake her head.

Then they clipped her claws carefully. They painted them pink to go with the bow tied around her neck.

Scat's meals were served in a silver bowl. She had beef and chicken and liver and cheese. She had milk and

cream. And every day she had to take vitamins.

But she never had any fish, and that's what she missed most of all. Soon Scat began playing in the movies. In her first picture she showed the FBI where a band of robbers was hiding. In another movie Scat jumped out of a burning building to go for help. And she danced with Miss DelRay in a musical called, *The Cat's Pajamas.*

Every Thursday night she was on television with a friendly poodle. The show was called "Scat & Pat."

Her pictures were in all the newspapers. There were stories about her in the magazines. She became known everywhere as Scat, the Movie Cat.

Gift shops sold Scat shirts and Scat ties. All over the country children were starting Scat clubs.

Back home, in Gull Harbor, Joel saw Scat on television programs. He went to the movies and saw her on the screen. He was proud of his movie cat.

But as the months passed, Joel missed her more and more. Six months went by, and still Mr. Wozel did not bring her back to Joel.

"I told you," said Granny. "Now that she's famous, you'll probably never see her again."

Yet month after month Joel waited for her. Each day he hoped Mr. Wozel would bring Scat home.

He never did.

Finally Joel could wait no longer. He sat down and wrote a letter.

Dear Miss DelRay,

I am happy that my cat is so famous. I am proud of her, too. But I wonder when she is coming home.

Mr. Wozel promised that Scat would be home in six months. Almost a year has passed, and I've heard nothing from him.

Would you tell Mr. Wozel that I am waiting? I miss Scat very much, and I am sure she misses me. I know you will understand.

Your friend,
Joel

One day Mr. Wozel brought Scat to the Paws and Claws. He gave her to the young lady for grooming. The lady put Scat in a box to wait her turn.

When no one was looking, Scat jumped out. While she was exploring, she met Blackie, a tomcat.

Scat and Blackie liked each other immediately. They romped about and rubbed cheeks. While the cats were playing, they found a door open at the back of the shop and dashed out into the street.

That night the news spread all over Film City. SCAT, THE MOVIE CAT, IS MISSING. Policemen, firemen, and even private detectives began looking for her.

Miss DelRay offered a $5,000 reward for her safe return.

As the weeks passed, Scat and Blackie found their way down to the railroad tracks. There Scat's beautiful brown coat became black with soot and coal dust. Many people saw her. But she was so dirty they did not know who she was.

There was a big black dog who lived in the freight yards. He belonged to the railway guard. Twice he chased Scat and Blackie. Each time they escaped by running under the station platform.

Scat and Blackie soon got used to the roar of the trains. They made a home in an old packing box near the railroad siding. From here they went out each night searching for food. There was not much to be found, and they often went hungry.

One night Scat and Blackie awoke later than usual. It was already dark. They stretched and yawned, and then started out on their nightly hunt.

They had only gone a short distance when Scat lifted her head and sniffed. She saw a moving shadow. Blackie saw it too. It was the big dog, and he was very close to them.

Blackie dashed back between the boxes. Scat waited a second too long. The dog caught her just as she started across the tracks. She spit and scratched, and finally the dog let go of her. Scat looked around frantically for a place to hide. There was a switch box on the tracks only a few inches away. Quickly Scat jumped into it.

The dog reached down with a paw and tried to catch Scat. She lay as low as she could in the box. The dog tried desperately to pull her out of the box. But Scat held on with all her might.

Just then Scat heard a loud whistle. The bright headlight of a train lighted up the night. The dog saw the light, too. Quickly he jumped out of the way. All Scat could do was to stay close to the ground.

A second later the big train roared right over her. She closed her eyes. The ground shook. Scat heard the grinding of the iron wheels only inches away. The noise and the wind made Scat shiver with fright.

The long train roared on and on over

the cat. Finally the last car went by. Scat jumped out from her hiding place and ran across the tracks. She hid again under the station platform.

It was a long time before Scat felt safe enough to come out. When she did, she tried to find Blackie. He seemed to have disappeared. For three days Scat searched and searched, but she never saw Blackie again.

It had been a long time since Scat had had a good meal. Now she was starving. She knew she must find food. As she looked, she suddenly smelled the odor of fish. It came from an open box-car. In the corner of the car Scat found some bits of fish. She ate them all up hungrily.

She was still in the car when suddenly the big door slammed shut behind her. Slowly the car started to move. The wheels clicked and clacked as the train chugged along the tracks. It went faster and faster.

There was a small crack in the door. Scat looked out, watching the fields and farmlands go by. She had no idea where she was or where she was going. She only knew she was cold and hungry.

For two days and nights the train rolled along. On the third day the car was dropped off on a siding. Then Scat heard the voices of workmen. Suddenly the door opened. The workmen started loading boxes of fish into the empty car.

Scat jumped out. She ran between the legs of the busy workmen.

"A black cat," shouted one of the workmen. "Watch out."

Scat saw an open truck. She climbed in and hid behind some empty boxes. The boxes smelled of fish and crabmeat.

The owner of the truck came along and climbed into the driver's seat. The truck started down the road. All morning it traveled along the highway. It crossed a bridge and pulled into a dockside.

After the owner walked away, Scat jumped out. Slowly she looked around. She saw the fishing boats tied to the dock. She saw the long wooden sheds of the market. They all looked familiar.

Scat started to walk down the road.

Soon she passed the ice-cream stand. She
walked faster and faster. She crossed
the little bridge.

Scat saw a boy sitting on the pier,
fishing. She knew that it was Joel. She
walked over and sat down beside him.

Joel looked at her and smiled. "Hello, cat," he said. "How would you like a fish?" He put a small hook on the end of the line. A few minutes later he pulled up a minnow.

Scat reached out for it with her paw.

Joel's eyes grew big with wonder. He patted the cat with his wet hands. Some of the soot and dirt came off on his fingers. Then he wet his hand again and rubbed her fur. This time more dirt came off. Now he saw the cat's brown fur and some of her stripes.

Joel picked the cat up in his arms. He ran as fast as he could. When he reached the little house, Joel shouted, "Granny, Granny."

Granny came out on the porch.

"It's Scat," he shouted. "It's Scat, and she's come home."

Granny smiled. The tears ran down her cheeks.

They rubbed Scat off with a towel. Then they could see the reddish brown fur and the beautiful black stripes. Next they gave Scat a big dish of sardines.

That afternoon Joel received a letter from Miss DelRay.

Dear Joel,

I am sure you must know that Scat ran away some time ago.

When your letter came I was angry and hurt to learn that Mr. Wozel had not been in touch with you. I cannot tell you how sorry I am.

I have bought your little cottage from Mr. Wozel. Now it belongs to you and Granny. I only hope this will make up for some of the sadness we have caused.

If we ever find Scat, I promise I will bring her home to you without delay.

Your friend,
Lily DelRay

Granny smiled. "Well, it looks like our troubles are over," she said. "We'll have to let Miss DelRay know that Scat has come home."

Joel was happy. "Tomorrow I'll take her fishing," he said. "She likes that best of all."

But the next day Scat could not go fishing. She was too busy taking care of her little family. During the night she had had a litter of five kittens, four black and one reddish brown with black stripes.

Joel held up the brown one. "When this kitten grows up," he said, "we'll send it to Miss DelRay."

"She'll be another Scat," said Granny. "I'm sure everyone will like that."